Rochelle
the Star Spotter
Fairy

To Isabella with lots of love

Special thanks to
Rachel Elliot

ORCHARD BOOKS
338 Euston Road, London NW1 3BH
Orchard Books Australia
Level 17/207 Kent Street, Sydney, NSW 2000
A Paperback Original

First published in 2012 by Orchard Books

HIT entertainment

A CIP catalogue record for this book is available
from the British Library.

ISBN 978 1 40831 594 1

1 3 5 7 9 10 8 6 4 2

Printed in Great Britain

The paper and board used in this paperback are natural recyclable
products made from wood grown in sustainable forests. The
manufacturing processes conform to the environmental regulations
of the country of origin.

Orchard Books is a division of Hachette Children's Books,
an Hachette UK company

www.hachette.co.uk

Rochelle
the Star Spotter
Fairy

by Daisy Meadows

ORCHARD

www.rainbowmagic.co.uk

Jack Frost's Spell

It's high time for the world to see
The legend I was born to be.
The prince of pop, a dazzling star
My fans will flock from near and far.

But pop star fame is hard to get
Unless I help myself, I bet.
I need a plan, a cunning trick
To make my stage act super-slick.

Seven magic clefs I'll steal
They'll give me pop star powers, I feel.
I'll sing and dance, I'll dazzle and shine
And pop star glory will be mine!

Contents

Showers and Sparkles

"Another gorgeous morning at the Rainspell Island Music Festival!" said Kirsty Tate happily. "Do you think I should wear this daisy headband today, Rachel?"

Her best friend Rachel Walker looked at their reflections in the big shower block mirror.

"Definitely!" she said with a smile. "The white petals look so pretty against your dark hair."

The girls had just finished showering and getting dressed. They were camping at the festival with Rachel's parents, and they were all special guests of The Angels pop group.

"I think you should wear my rose headband," Kirsty said, handing it to Rachel. "It will really suit you."

"I feel so lucky to be here," said Rachel as she arranged the headband in her hair. "I've lost count of all the amazing things we've done – and the fabulous concerts we've been to!"

"As well as the fun we've had helping the fairies," said Kirsty with a twinkle in her eye.

No one knew that the girls were friends with the people of Fairyland. They had often helped the fairies to outwit grumpy Jack Frost and his mischievous goblins. Soon after they arrived on Rainspell Island, they had met the Pop Star Fairies, who used their magical clef necklaces to look after pop music. Jack Frost and his goblins had stolen the clefs and brought them to the festival to help Jack become a pop star. So far, Kirsty and Rachel had helped five of the Pop Star Fairies to find their magic clefs.

"I just hope that we can find the two missing clefs before the end of the festival," said Rachel.

"Me too," said Kirsty. "It would be terrible if Jack Frost managed to ruin it for everyone. There are still lots of fantastic concerts to look forward to."

"Yes, I can't wait to see Jacob Bright at the Talent of Tomorrow show later," said Rachel. "He's one of the biggest up-and-coming stars here."

"And we still haven't seen Jax Tempo perform," said Kirsty. "I wonder when he'll be on stage. He must be very good to get so famous so quickly – I hadn't even heard of him until the start of the festival."

"Well, I'm ready," said Rachel. "Let's get our things and go back to the tent."

Kirsty put her hairbrush and spare hairbands back into her sponge bag, while Rachel went into the shower cubicle to get her shampoo.

But as she leaned over
the shower tray,
she noticed that the
remaining bubbles
were sparkling with
rainbow colours.
Rachel felt a
prickle of excitement
running up and down
her spine.

"Kirsty!" she called. "Come
over here. I think something magical is
about to happen!"

Kirsty hurried eagerly into the cubicle,
carrying her sponge bag and towel. The
girls watched as the glistening foam
grew fluffier and more colourful. Then
there was a burst of miniature suds, and
a tiny fairy fluttered out of them.

"It's Rochelle
the Star Spotter
Fairy!" said
Rachel with
a beaming
smile. "Hello,
it's great to
see you!"

"Hello, Rachel!
Hello, Kirsty!"
said Rochelle. "I'm so
relieved that I've found you! I've been
searching everywhere for my musical clef
necklace – will you help me get it back
from Jack Frost and his goblins?"

Rochelle gazed at them hopefully
through her stylish glasses. Her
silver-grey dress shimmered in the electric
lights of the shower cubicle.

"We'd love to," said Kirsty.

"Of course!" added Rachel.

"Thank you!" said Rochelle, clapping her hands together. "You see, my clef helps people to have confidence in front of an audience. If I don't find it soon, the pop stars at the festival will be too shy to perform."

"Oh no!" said Kirsty. "If the stars can't perform, there won't be any concerts. The festival will be spoiled."

"Not only that," said Rochelle in a worried voice, "without my clef, new pop talent across the human world will never be spotted."

Before the girls could reply, they heard the shower block door opening. Someone was coming in!

Voice of an Angel

Quickly, Rochelle darted into Kirsty's sponge bag. She was only just in time! A girl with dark curly hair walked past the open door of the cubicle where the girls were standing. She was carrying a blue bag that said 'HOLLY' on the side in white embroidered letters. She gave the girls a shy smile and went into a shower cubicle.

"Let's go," Rachel whispered. "We need to find somewhere private where we can talk to Rochelle."

Rachel picked up her sponge bag and

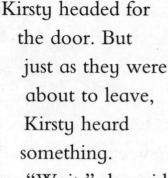 towel, and she and Kirsty headed for the door. But just as they were about to leave, Kirsty heard something.

"Wait," she said. "Listen."

From the cubicle that Holly had walked into, there came a faint but beautiful sound. At first the girls could hardly make out the words over the sound of the shower. But gradually the singing grew louder.

"That's an Angels song – *Key to My Heart*!" Rachel exclaimed. "Do you remember the first time we heard it, Kirsty?"

"Of course I do," said Kirsty, smiling at her best friend. "It was at The Angels' charity concert, when we were helping Destiny the Pop Star Fairy."

Holly's voice grew even louder and more confident.

"Wow!" said Rachel. "Holly's voice is amazing! She sounds like a real pop star."

21

They listened, entranced, until the song ended and the shower was turned off. Kirsty and Rachel burst into applause.

"You've got an incredible voice!" said Kirsty. "I've never heard anyone sing like that before. You're wonderful!"

"Oh, thanks," said Holly, suddenly sounding very shy.

The girls heard her getting dressed. Then she came out, drying her long dark hair with a towel.

"Are you going to sing in the Talent of Tomorrow show later?" Rachel asked. "I hope so – I can't wait to hear you sing again!"

A delicate blush rose in Holly's cheeks.

"I don't think so," she said. "I love singing, but not for an audience. It's too embarrassing."

"But you sang just now with us listening," Kirsty said.

"I thought you were leaving," Holly said. "I couldn't possibly perform on a stage in front of hundreds of people. I'd be too scared!"

Before the girls could try to persuade her any further, Holly hurried past them and left the shower block. The girls stared at each other in surprise.

"I wish she could realise how good she really is," said Rachel.

"Me too," Kirsty replied. "But right now we have to help Rochelle. Come on!"

They raced back to their tent and dropped off their shower things. Mr and Mrs Walker were making a cup of tea on their little camping stove.

"Having a good time, girls?" asked Mr Walker, smiling at them.

"Yes thanks, Dad," said Rachel, edging in front of her best friend.

Quickly, Kirsty opened her sponge bag. Rochelle zoomed up and hid under her hair.

"OK," Kirsty whispered to Rachel.

"See you later," called Rachel, waving at her parents.

"Are you off again?" said Mrs Walker with a laugh. "Have fun!"

The best friends walked away from the tents and across the grass towards the outdoor concert stage. "It'll be quiet there," said Kirsty. "We can talk in private and make a plan to find Rochelle's missing clef."

But when they arrived at the stage, they found that it was already quite busy. The Angels were there to prepare for the Talent of Tomorrow concert, and there were runners and technicians working busily all around.

26

"We should tell The Angels about Holly," said Rachel. "Maybe they can persuade her to sing later."

"If Holly's going to have the confidence to sing for the audience, we need my magic clef back," said Rochelle from her hiding place. "Otherwise no one will be able to make her sing – not even The Angels."

As the girls neared the stage, they heard a soft voice singing in the wings.

"*Sing it loud, sing it proud,*
Sing for everyone to hear..."

"I know that voice!" Kirsty gasped. "It's Jacob Bright!"

The Green Guy Trio

The girls peeped into the wings. The handsome young singer was standing alone, practising his new hit, *Sing It*. But his voice was so soft that the girls could hardly hear him.

Just then he glimpsed Rachel and Kirsty, and stopped singing at once.

"Hello," said Rachel in excitement. "You're one of our favourite pop stars! We love your music!"

Jacob Bright blushed red in embarrassment and turned away, mumbling something.

"That's odd," said Kirsty under her breath. "I wouldn't have thought such a big star would be so shy."

Just then, they heard someone calling their names. They turned around to see The Angels waving at them.

"Hello!" said Emilia, coming over and giving them a big hug. "How lovely to see you here!"

"Are you getting ready for the Talent of Tomorrow concert?" Rachel asked. "We're really looking forward to it!"

The Angels looked at each other.

"I'm afraid we don't even know if there's going to *be* a concert," said Serena, her forehead creasing into a frown.

"What do you mean?" asked Kirsty. "Can't you decide which singers to include?"

"Oh, I wish we had *that* problem," said Lexy. "This is far worse. Not one single person has signed up!"

"But there must be lots of people at the festival who want to be pop stars," said Rachel in astonishment.

"That's what we thought," said Serena with a sigh. "Perhaps we were wrong."

"No, you weren't wrong," Kirsty exclaimed. "We met a girl today with a really beautiful voice... she was just too shy to sing at the concert."

"Listen, I bet you two are great at spotting talent," said Emilia. "Would you look around the festival for us and try to find some budding pop stars?"

"We'd love to!" said Rachel.

"Thanks, girls," said Serena. "Come and find us later, and tell us who you've discovered!"

Rachel and Kirsty headed towards Star Village, the festival's cluster of activity tents.

"I'm so excited about talent-spotting for The Angels!" said Kirsty. "Rochelle, we're lucky to have you here – you'll be able to help us look for stars, and we can search for your clef at the same time!"

"I'd love to," said Rochelle. "Star spotting is my favourite thing!"

As soon as the girls walked into Star Village, they saw a young boy doing some street dancing beside the make-up tent. He was singing a cool hip-hop tune and practising impressive shoulder pops and head spins. A few people had noticed him and were starting to gather round.

"He's got real potential," whispered Rochelle.

But just then the boy noticed the little crowd around him. He stopped and stared down at the ground, shuffling his feet together.

"Don't stop!" called out a girl in the crowd. "That was brilliant!"

"Yes, we really liked it," said Rachel. "Please carry on – we're looking for people to perform at the Talent of Tomorrow concert."

"No way!" said the boy, looking scared. "I couldn't do that." He sidled away, and the three friends sighed. Everywhere they looked, they found the same story. Near the Food Fest area, a girl was strumming her guitar beautifully. But as soon as they drew closer, she put it down. People were singing, dancing and playing instruments all over Star Village, but none of them wanted to perform in the talent concert.

"This is terrible," said Kirsty. "No one wants to perform at the concert – and there is no sign of Rochelle's magical clef either."

"We'll have to go and tell The Angels," said Rachel. "I hate to disappoint them."

They walked slowly back to the stage. The Angels were still there, but this time they looked much happier. Jacob Bright was there too, smiling broadly.

"Girls, we've found an act for the talent show!" called Serena when she saw them. "They're absolutely fantastic – The Green Guy Trio!"

Up on the stage, three singers were
confidently performing a show tune.
They were all dressed in bright green
polo shirts, checked trousers and woollen
tam o'shanter caps with large peaks that
covered their faces. Each of them had
a few moments in the spotlight, then
gave a high-five hand-slap to the next
member so that he could take his turn.

"At least there's one act for the Talent of Tomorrow concert," said Rochelle.

Rachel was staring at the band's huge shiny green shoes.

"How can they dance wearing those enormous shoes?" she wondered aloud.

"That's funny," said Kirsty. "I think they're passing something to each other when they do their high-fives."

"Let me take a look," said Rochelle.

Keeping out of sight, she fluttered closer to the band. Then she came zooming back to the girls, her eyes wide.

"Rachel! Kirsty!" she gasped. "They've got my magical clef!"

"Oh my goodness!" said Rachel. "The Green Guy Trio are really green *goblins*!"

Tricks
and Treats

The goblins' song ended, and suddenly,
there was a commotion backstage. The
girls could hear someone shouting.

"I'll make you sorry you ever clapped
eyes on that clef!" snarled the voice.

Then the rising star Jax Tempo
appeared on stage, his fists clenched in
rage. He stomped towards the goblins,
who scrambled off the stage as fast as
they could. Jax Tempo's ice-blue suit
glittered in the sunshine.

"Get back here, you bunch of blundering brainless blockheads!" he roared. "I'm the one meant for pop stardom, not you! Give me that clef NOW!"

He stormed after them and the girls stared open-mouthed. They would have recognised that spiky hair and bad temper anywhere. Jax Tempo was really Jack Frost in disguise!

"We have to get the magical clef from the goblins before Jack Frost does," said Rochelle in a panic. "Girls, it'll be easier if you're both fairies as well."

Rachel and Kirsty nodded and looked around. The Angels were deep in conversation with Jacob Bright, and none of the technicians was looking their way.

"Let's go behind the stage curtain," said Kirsty. "No one will see us there."

The girls hurried up onto the stage and ducked behind the spangled blue curtain. Then Rochelle flew out from under the daisy on Kirsty's headband, already waving her wand. Rainbow sparkles erupted from the tip of her wand, engulfing the girls in a glittering puff of colour.

Instantly they shrank to fairy-size and
flapped their gossamer wings, twirling
into the air in delight.

"Follow me!" called
Rochelle.

Together,
the girls and
Rochelle flew
high above
the festival.
It was fun to look
down on the tents and crowds below, all
spread out like a living, moving map.

"I hope that no one looks up and sees
us," said Kirsty.

"We're so high up that we will look
like tiny dots to them," said Rochelle
with a smile. "We'll have to be careful
when we fly down again, though."

"There's Jack Frost!" exclaimed Rochelle.

She pointed to the crowds who were milling around Star Village. In the midst of the festival-goers, they could see Jack Frost's ice-blue suit glittering like a beacon. He was still stomping around, looking for the goblins and the magical clef.

"I'm glad he's wearing that suit," said Rachel. "It makes him very easy to spot, and there are lots of people dressed up here so no one thinks he looks odd."

"If only the goblins were that easy to follow," said Kirsty. "How are we going to find them in all these crowds? We don't even know which one of them has the clef."

"Wait a minute!" said Rachel. "Listen – can you hear someone singing?"

The three friends hovered in midair, listening. Above the cheerful buzz of the festival noise, they could hear a loud, tuneful singing voice.

"That's Jacob Bright's song, *Sing It*!" said Kirsty, remembering how they had heard him practising in the stage wings.

"The only person who would have the confidence to sing that loud at the moment is the one with my clef," said Rochelle. "If we follow that sound, I'm sure it will lead us to the goblins!"

They zigzagged through the air, letting the sound guide them. They were led to the Food Fest picnic area, and then Rachel gave a shout.

"There they are!" she said, pointing to three figures in green.

The goblins were taking turns singing and dancing in the shade of a leafy tree. They were still passing the magical clef necklace to each other with their high-fives.

Rachel, Kirsty and Rochelle fluttered lower. All the people in the area were busy enjoying their picnics, and no one was looking up. They concealed themselves in the leaves of the tree above the goblins.

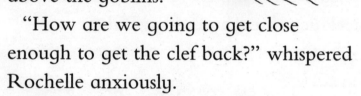

"How are we going to get close enough to get the clef back?" whispered Rochelle anxiously.

"These picnickers have given me an idea," said Kirsty. "Rochelle, could you magic up a feast fit for a pop star? Goblins are always hungry. I could be disguised as a server, and try to get the clef back."

"Good plan, Kirsty!" said Rachel.

Rochelle waved her wand and a jet of fairy dust spiralled through the air. It hit the ground on the other side of the tree from the goblins, and instantly a heavily laden table sprang up. It looked and smelled delicious. There were colourful cupcakes on tiered holders, a bowl of fizzy green fruit punch and an enormous Victoria sponge topped with strawberries and cream.

"Now it's my turn," said Kirsty. "Wish me luck!"

Pesky Fairies!

Kirsty fluttered down beside the table, and with another wave of Rochelle's wand she was transformed into a server from a Food Fest stall, wearing a black dress and a little white apron. Rachel and Rochelle flew down and hid behind the large punch bowl. At that moment, the wonderful food smells reached the goblins' noses, and three green faces peered around the tree.

"Are you The Green Guy Trio?" asked Kirsty in a cheerful voice. "We've set up a special feast for you, paid for by the talent show organisers."

"Yes!" shouted the goblins, scrambling over each other towards the tempting food.

As they greedily shoved cupcakes into their mouths, Kirsty took a step closer.

"Um, I was wondering if you would sing for me," she asked. "Everyone says that you've got amazing voices, but I haven't heard you yet."

Hidden behind the punch bowl, Rochelle and Rachel were listening to every word.

"That's a clever idea," whispered Rochelle. "Whichever goblin is willing to sing for her must have my magical clef!"

Eager to show off, one goblin started singing. He sounded like a pop star!

"He's the one!" said Rochelle.

She and Rachel zoomed out of their hiding place towards the goblin. They could see the magical clef clutched in his hand! But just as Rachel was reaching out to touch it, one of the other goblins gave a squawk of alarm.

"Fairies!" he yelled. "Yucky, tricksy, pesky fairies!"

Quickly, the singing goblin threw the clef to him, and they both ran off through the festival. The third goblin was too busy munching on the Victoria sponge cake to bother giving chase.

Kirsty ran after the two disappearing goblins, leaving the third one to enjoy the feast. Rachel and Rochelle zoomed overhead, trying to keep the goblins in sight.

"They're heading for Star Village,"
said Rachel. "I've got an idea!"

She and Rochelle
swooped down and
tucked themselves
under Kirsty's hair.

"Listen,"
said Rachel
breathlessly. "The
goblins love being
flattered. Let's
dress up as fans of
The Green Guy Trio —
they're bound to let us get close to them
and we might be able to get the magic
clef back."

"I think that could work," said
Rochelle. "But we'll have to be out of
sight for me to do my magic."

Kirsty darted behind a deserted tent, and Rachel and Rochelle flew out. The little fairy waved her wand at her human friends and chanted a spell.

"Help me foil the goblins' plans.
Make these girls true Green Guys fans!"

A jet of green fairy dust instantly transformed Rachel and Kirsty! Rachel grew back to her normal size, and both girls found themselves wearing green dresses and green tam o'shanters. Kirsty had a little video camera in her hand.

"We look just like fans!" said Rachel with a giggle. "Now we just have to find the goblins."

Rochelle hid in Rachel's pocket, and then the girls ran through Star Village. Almost immediately they spotted a flash of green in the crowd. The two goblins were hurrying along.

"Keep a lookout for fairies!" they heard the taller one say.

"It's The Green Guy Trio!" squealed Kirsty at the top of her voice.

"Stop!" shrieked Rachel. "We're your biggest fans!"

They raced after the goblins, who
stopped and grinned at them in delight.
"Can we video you?" asked Kirsty,
holding up the camera.
"This is very
exciting!"
"Sure," said
the taller
goblin with a
little swagger.
"Anything for
our fans."
Rachel posed
beside the two
preening goblins as
Kirsty filmed them.
"It would be so cool to get you singing
on tape," said Rachel. "Please would
you sing for the video?"

Eagerly, the shorter goblin took a step forward and launched into *Sing It*. He must have the clef! Rochelle flitted out from Rachel's pocket to get it, but the tip of her wing brushed against the goblin's arm.

On the alert for fairies, the goblin gave a squawk and darted off into the crowd, without even waiting to tell his companion why he had run away.

"Hey!" the taller goblin shouted after him.

"Never mind him!" said Kirsty quickly. "Everyone knows that you're the real star of the band!"

The goblin smiled smugly. Because of the video camera, a small crowd had started to gather, thinking that he must really be famous. The girls were able to slip away without him noticing.

"We have to catch up with that goblin," said Rachel. "If Jack Frost finds him first, we could lose the clef forever!"

As soon as they were out of sight, Rochelle turned Kirsty and Rachel back into fairies again. They zoomed up into the air and looked around.

"I see him!" cried Kirsty. "He's heading towards the campsite!"

They chased the goblin towards the field full of little tents. Luckily it wasn't very busy, because most people were exploring the festival. The goblin dodged between the tents and the girls darted after him. Somewhere nearby they could hear someone singing. It sounded like Holly!

The goblin was a very fast runner, and the girls were getting tired. Just then, Rachel gave a cry of alarm and pointed into the distance. Someone was striding towards the campsite in an ice-blue suit that glittered. He had spiky hair, and he was clenching his fists.

"It's Jack Frost!" exclaimed Kirsty. "And he's looking for the goblin!"

Jack Frost Goes Goblin-Hunting

The goblin spotted Jack Frost at exactly the same moment. He froze in his tracks and started to shake. The girls caught up with him and he looked at them with big, scared eyes.

"Don't let him find me!" he squeaked. "He's going to be so cross, and I hate it when he shouts!"

Even though the goblin had been very naughty, the girls felt sorry for him.

"Our tent is very close by," said
Rachel. "You can hide in there if
you like."

"Yes!" said the goblin. "Quick, hide
me, please!"

He was too frightened of Jack Frost to
worry about the fairies now.

Rachel and Kirsty flitted ahead and led
him to their tent.

"I hope Mum and Dad are out," said
Rachel.

Luckily, the tent
was empty. The
goblin scurried
inside and the
three friends
swooped after
him and zipped
the tent flap shut.

The goblin sat down in the middle of the tent. Outside, they could hear Jack Frost getting closer.

"I know that goblin came this way," they heard him muttering. "I saw his footprints. I'm going to search every single tent until I find him, and then I'll make him sorry he stole from me!"

When he heard this, the goblin started shaking again. Bravely, Rachel flew over to him and perched on his knee.

"Listen to me, goblin," she said. "We can help you escape. Rochelle can use her magic to send you to the other end of the festival grounds. But if you want our help, you have to help us too. Give back the magical clef necklace. It doesn't belong to you."

The goblin thought about it for a moment.

"If I give you the necklace, you'll help me escape?" he asked.

The three little fairies nodded. Outside, Jack Frost's stomping footsteps were getting louder.

"All right!" squawked the goblin. "I'll do it."

He thrust the clef towards Rochelle, and it immediately shrank to fairy-size.

"You've done the right thing," Kirsty promised the goblin.

"I don't care about that," he snapped. "Just get me out of here!"

Rochelle waved her wand. In a rainbow-coloured flash, the goblin disappeared to the other end of the festival – just as the tent flap was whipped open. Jack Frost's furious face appeared in the entrance.

67

"You're too late," said Rachel, putting her hands on her hips. "Rochelle's got her clef back."

"You set of interfering wretches!" Jack Frost screeched. "You'll be sorry you've crossed my path! I've still got the last clef, and that means I can ruin your precious concert tomorrow – and all concerts everywhere!"

Giving them a final scowl, he disappeared in a bolt of icy lightning.

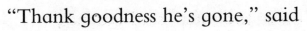

"Thank goodness he's gone," said
Kirsty with a sigh.

"You have both
been amazing,"
said Rochelle,
hugging
them tightly.
"Thank you
for getting my
clef back. Now
you'll be able to
enjoy the Talent of
Tomorrow concert – my clef will give
the singers the courage to perform!"

She returned them to human-size and
fastened the clef around her neck.

"I'm going back to Fairyland to tell the
other Pop Star Fairies the good news,"
she said.

"Goodbye, Rochelle!" said the girls. "It was fun star-spotting with you!"

At the Talent of Tomorrow show that evening, the atmosphere was electric. All the talented performers that the girls had spotted earlier had signed up for the show. Rachel and Kirsty were in the front row with Rachel's parents. They cheered and clapped for the hip-hop artist and the guitar player. The audience was on its feet, whistling and whooping. The Angels walked onstage to introduce the next act.

"Now we're delighted to present a duo that'll rock your world," said Emilia.

"That's right," Lexy added. "These guys sound awesome individually, but together they're dynamite."

"And you're lucky enough to be here for their first duet," said Serena. "Go wild for Jacob Bright... and Holly Day!"

Spotlights swept across the stage and fireworks exploded in time to the music. Jacob and Holly walked out side by side, and launched into Jacob's latest hit.

Everyone listened as Holly's voice soared out, clear and confident.

"What an amazing voice!" exclaimed Mrs Walker. "She's definitely a star in the making."

"I think Mum wants to be a star spotter too," said Rachel with a giggle. She and Kirsty raised their arms in the air and swayed as they sang along to the chorus:

"Sing it loud, sing it proud,
Sing for everyone to hear..."

Just then, something made Rachel turn around. A few rows behind them, she saw the three goblins in their Green Guy Trio outfits, arms raised and swaying. She nudged Kirsty, who looked back and smiled.

"They seem to be enjoying themselves too much to cause any mischief at the moment," she said.

The event was a huge success. But Rachel and Kirsty knew that Una the Concert Fairy's magical clef was still missing. It was up to them to get it back from Jack Frost and his goblins – or the festival finale would be ruined!

**Now Kirsty and Rachel
must help...**

Una the Concert Fairy

Read on for a sneak peek...

"My autograph book is almost full,"
said Kirsty Tate, turning the blue pages
happily. "We've met so many famous
pop stars at the festival!"

"Mine too," said Rachel Walker, who
had her pink autograph book open on
her lap. "I can't believe it's our last day
already."

"The Rainspell Island Music Festival
has been so much fun, I can hardly
imagine going back to ordinary life,"
said Kirsty with a laugh. "I wish it didn't
have to end."

Kirsty and Rachel were sitting on camping stools outside their tent. They had really enjoyed being special guests of their favourite pop group, The Angels. The afternoon sun seemed to light up the tents around them with a golden glow.

"It looks as if it's enchanted, doesn't it?" said Rachel. "Almost as magical as the fairy campsite we visited with Jessie the Lyrics Fairy."

Kirsty and Rachel were good friends with many fairies, and they had often visited Fairyland and thwarted Jack Frost's schemes. On the first day of the festival, they had stumbled across one of his most mischievous plans yet. The Ice Lord had stolen seven magical clef necklaces from the Pop Star Fairies to try to become a pop star himself.

He had given most of the clefs to his goblins, who brought them to the Rainspell Island Festival, where Kirsty and Rachel had been able to track them down one by one. Jack Frost had disguised himself as rapper Jax Tempo to impress people at the festival, but he didn't fool the girls for long.

The Pop Star Fairies needed their clefs to look after all aspects of pop music, and Kirsty and Rachel were determined to help their friends. So far, they had helped six fairies get their magic clefs back, but Jack Frost still had one. It belonged to Una the Concert Fairy...

Read Una the Concert Fairy to find out what adventures are in store for Kirsty and Rachel!

Meet the
Pop Star Fairies

Jessie
the Lyrics
Fairy

Adele
the Singing Coach
Fairy

Out
Apr
Vanessa
the Dance Steps
Fairy

Miley
the Stylist
Fairy

Frankie
the Make-up
Fairy

Rochelle
the Star Spotter
Fairy

Out
Jun
Una
the Concert
Fairy

Kirsty and Rachel have to save Rainspell Island Music
Festival after Jack Frost steals the Pop Star Fairies'
musical clef necklaces!

www.rainbowmagicbooks.co.uk

Competition!

Here's a friend who Kirsty and Rachel met in an earlier story. Use the clues below to help you guess her name. When you have enjoyed all seven of the Pop Star Fairies books, arrange the first letters of each mystery fairy's name to make a special word, then send us the answer!

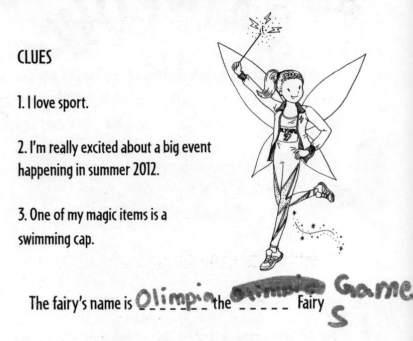

CLUES

1. I love sport.

2. I'm really excited about a big event happening in summer 2012.

3. One of my magic items is a swimming cap.

The fairy's name is O̲l̲i̲m̲p̲i̲a̲ the O̲l̲i̲m̲p̲i̲c̲ G̲a̲m̲e̲s̲ Fairy

We will put all of the correct entries into a draw and select one winner to receive a special Pop Star Fairies goody bag. Your name will also be featured in a forthcoming Rainbow Magic story!

Enter online now at www.rainbowmagicbooks.co.uk